ACROSS THE RIVER

Walter & Oliver's Amazing Adventure:
A Tale of Persistence

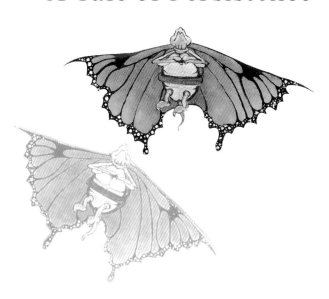

ACROSS THE RIVER

Walter & Oliver's Amazing Adventure:
A Tale of Persistence

•

BY D. MICHAEL PRICE

THE GREENWICH WORKSHOP PRESS

"**C**ome on, hurry up!" called Oliver Marsh to his older brother. The morning mist drifted gently through the roots and reeds as he headed toward the old swamp trail.

"Wait, I need my fishing hat," replied Walter as he pulled it from the dozens of hats hanging on the rack. Walter had a hat for just about any occasion.

The day began just as it always did in the Rockabout Hills— a misty morning sunrise followed by another beautiful day. As the boys made their way down the trail, a few bees buzzed lazily through the early sunlight.

Indeed, nothing seemed out of the ordinary. But that, of course, is exactly the kind of day when adventures happen.

The two had been fishing for hours with not even a minnow to show for it. The summer sun rose hot and shimmered in rays through the trees. An orange-footed grumpy dozed on a branch above them as Oliver tangled his line yet again.

Quite suddenly, as they often do, a dragonfly appeared out of nowhere. He carried a letter marked URGENT. He handed it to Walter and disappeared as quickly as he had come. The message was from their cousin Jerome.

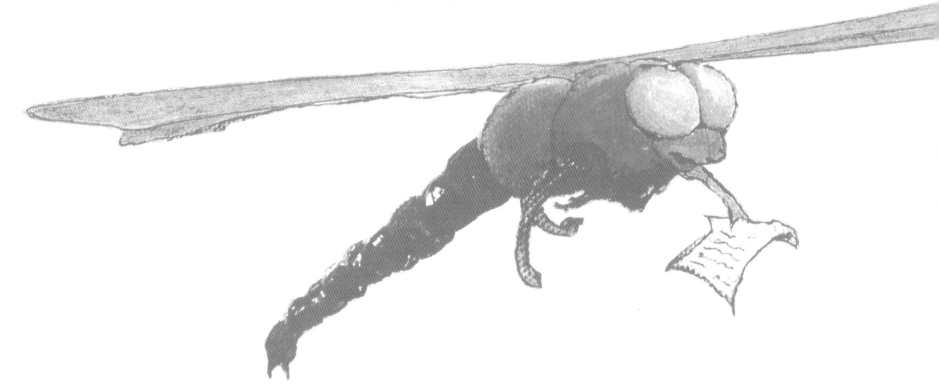

The message went like this: "To Oliver and Walter — It is most urgent that you find a way to get across the river to my house by tomorrow. Please hurry! Your cousin, Jerome."

He had drawn a map at the bottom of the page.

"Good heavens!" cried Walter. "Could he be in trouble?"

"We've never been to Jerome's, but we must go at once," said Oliver, looking brave.

"Yes, you're quite right," answered Walter. He wished he could put on a hat for bravery.

They were so distracted by Jerome's letter that their piscatorial pursuits were completely forgotten. This was all right, for although the two were terrible fishermen, they were *persistent,* and that would help them later on.

The best thing about worms for bait is that if you don't catch any fish, at least you can eat the worms. So after a fine dinner of worms and vegetables, the brothers walked down to the river.

At the water's edge, they could see the rock formation that Jerome had drawn on the map. They could also see that getting there would be another thing altogether.

"I don't know," said Oliver nervously. "The river is much too wide, too deep, and too fast for stepping stones."

"And besides," added Walter with disappointment, "we're land turtles. We can't swim that far anyway."

Perplexed, they began to walk back home as the twilight deepened.

Twilight is the magic time, being neither night nor day, but a little of both. Concerned about the problem before them, Oliver and Walter didn't notice the forest getting dark around them as they trudged home. Suddenly, a sparkling tumble of light and color went streaking past.

"Wow!" cried Walter. "It's the fairies!" And indeed it was the fairies of the wood. They were just starting a game of hide and seek.

"Please, join us," the fairies asked their friends the Marsh brothers, as they flew off giggling.

After much fun at hide and seek, which the fairies were very good at, they all roasted marshmallows and told stories. The fairies listened with interest as Walter told them about the urgent message from Jerome.

"If we had wings like you," Walter said, "we could fly right across the river!"

This sent the fairies into gales of laughter. "Turtles with wings!" they all cried together. "Whoever heard of such a thing?"

"Oh, please, can you help us?" asked the boys sadly, as they started for home once again. It was late, and they needed rest.

"Try to get a good night's sleep," said the fairies. "Perhaps we can think of something."

The kindness of fairies is legendary, and after a short discussion, the wee folk came up with a plan.

As the shadows of the night engulfed them, Luna, the leader of the fairies, was busy with the details of her creation. By midnight, the fairies' magic was complete.

The next morning, a wonderful surprise greeted the brothers when they woke up.

"Look at that!" shouted Oliver excitedly. "Hang gliders! The fairies have made hang gliders for us!"

Walter was nervous, but they agreed that it was worth the risk. And if they were persistent, they would learn how to fly the gliders, and soar across the river to where they hoped Jerome would be waiting.

liver and Walter wrote a nice thank-you note to the fairies and sent it off by Dragonfly Express. Then the two turtles turned their attention to learning how to fly the gliders.

Oliver, being the bolder of the two, volunteered to do the first test flights.

"Be careful, Oliver," called his brother.

"I'll try," Oliver said as he took a running jump off the edge of the stump.

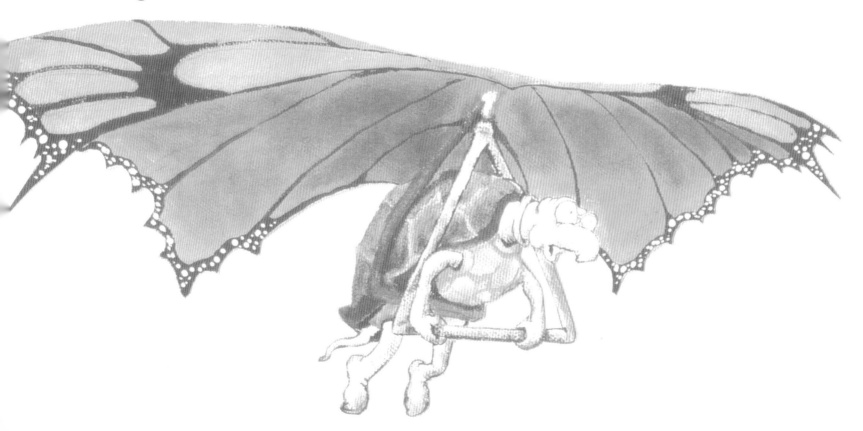

The gliders were magic, but the boys were not. As a result, Oliver met with various degrees of success. But sometimes you have to crash if you want to be good. After a couple of face plants, Oliver's hard work paid off, and he got the hang of it.

"It's wonnnnderrfulll!" he squealed with glee to Walter as he swooped past his brother.

Oliver proved to be excellent at flying his glider. Walter was nervous but determined, and soon Oliver taught him the technique.

"This is great!" he shouted to his younger brother. Soon both boys were soaring all about the forest.

Walter, remembering his brother's early tumbles, landed slowly and neatly a couple of times, just for practice.

"Let's go," he said. "I'm ready, I guess."

"You really should practice a little more," suggested Oliver.

"Let's just do it," replied Walter. He was still a little anxious about flying all the way across the river. "Let's get this over with," he thought to himself.

With a little help from their friends Hank and Frank, the leaping lizards, the boys got the hang gliders over to a rocky ledge by the river. The air here was much different than the forest air. The sky was bright, and it was windier in the wide-open spaces near the water.

"Ready?" asked Oliver.

"No, but we must go," was Walter's reply.

So they checked the wind and checked their map. They checked their gliders one last time, and with shouts of good luck from their friends, they were off…

As soon as the two little turtles leapt into the air, the wind caught their wings and lifted them high above the water. At first, they were nervous. But as the wind rushed past them and the opposite shore drew closer, the thrill of the adventure swept over them.

"This is amazing," Walter yelled as he flew by a very surprised orange-footed grumpy.

Walter and Oliver were halfway across the river, and everything was going great. They could see the rock formation that Jerome had drawn on the map, and they flew towards it.

"I can't believe I was ever afraid," Walter hollered as he sailed past his little brother.

"Don't be a daredevil," advised Oliver.

And then it happened. Just as they reached the other side of the river, a powerful updraft caught both of them. Oliver, who had a little more practice, soon regained control of his glider and watched helplessly as Walter was swept up...and up...and up.

"Walter, Walter!" yelled Oliver. "Hold tight, and don't let it spin." But Walter was so high above him, he never heard a word. He had never been anywhere near that high up. He also hadn't practiced as much as his brother, and he didn't know what to do as his glider began to spin. As he panicked, the spin turned to a fall, and Walter was thrown from his glider.

As he fell toward the trees, Walter had time to remember an old joke: It's not the fall that hurts; it's the sudden stop. He wasn't laughing when he hit the first branch.

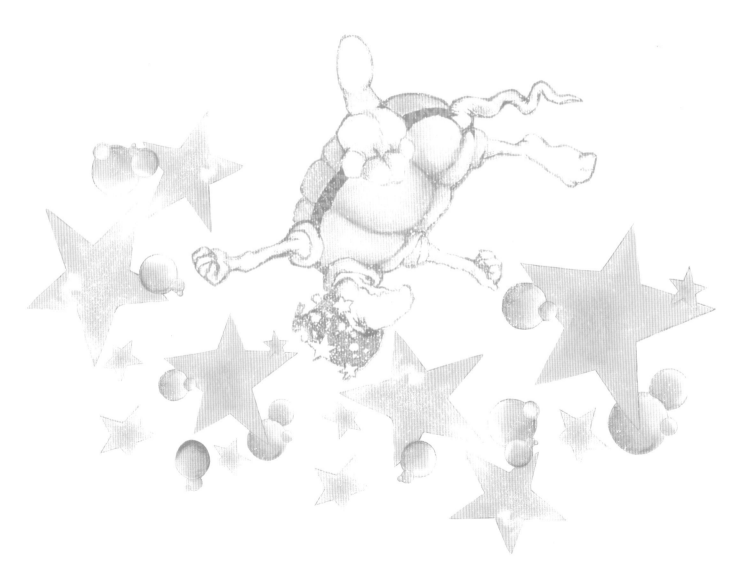

Walter continued on through the leaves. They slowed him down slightly, but not that much. When he collided with the second branch, he was very glad that a turtle's whole body is one big crash helmet.

By the time he hit the third branch, Walter had experienced all the crashing that anyone—even a hard-shelled turtle—could take.

Then, with a flash like black lightning, everything went dark. Walter had come to the end of his fall.

When Walter awoke, he thought, "Maybe I'm in heaven." He was cozy and warm. And it was nice and soft all around him. A wonderful, sweet smell greeted him, and a light seemed to be shining from somewhere above him.

When he stood up, he heard the voices.

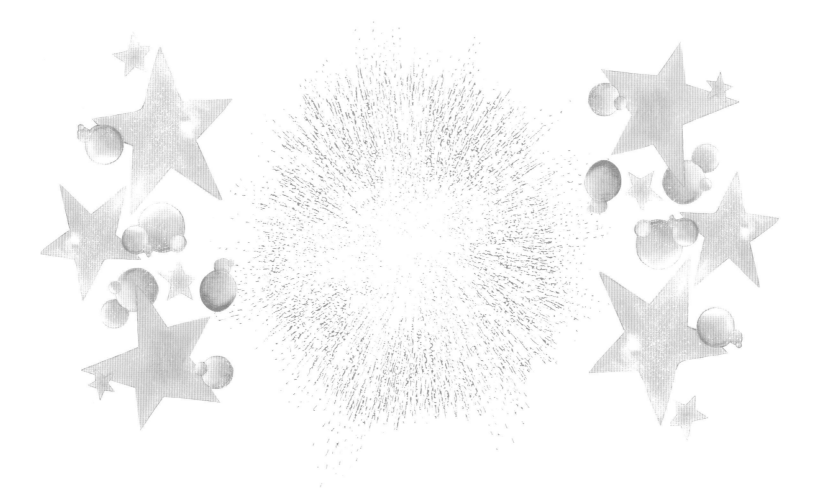

"Surprise!" they all shouted.

"Thank goodness you're all right, Walter!" laughed Oliver. "We were so worried about Jerome, we forgot that today is your birthday!"

To his delight, Walter had crash-landed into the cake of his own surprise party. He rubbed his eyes. There stood his cousin Jerome and all his friends, laughing and shouting, "Happy Birthday!"

It was one of the greatest parties ever thrown in the Rockabout Hills. They had root beer, corn on the cob, and marshmallows. They also had what was left of the birthday cake and, of course, lots of worms.

The brothers became famous for their feats of daring in the local skies. In fact, if you're out in the Rockabout Hills and you see a pair of butterflies, look closely. They may not be butterflies at all, but Oliver and Walter on their way to another adventure!

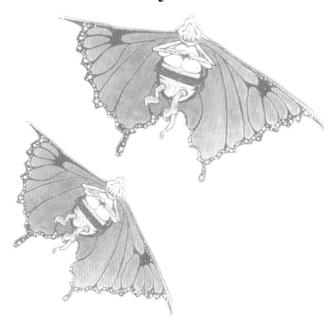